Home Sweet Home

Written and illustrated by
Shoo Rayner

RIGBY

Elno had grey feathers, with six dark spots.
His beak was black and his legs were pink.
"Elno is just too grey," the birds said.

Elno was shy.

All day long, he hid in a hole in a tree.

"Elno is just too shy," the birds said.

When all the birds were asleep,
Elno came out of his hole.
He cleared up the mess and then
went back into his hole.

The birds didn't see Elno and soon
they forgot about him.

One day, Elno flapped his wings and
flew away.
"No one wants me here.
I'll go and find a new home,"
he thought.

Elno flew across the world looking for a new home.

The desert was too hot.

The mountains were too high.

The city was too loud.

The sea was too wet.

But Elno liked the jungle.

The jungle birds were bright with colours.

Rose red.

Sunshine yellow.

Sky blue.

Jungle green.

And when the jungle birds saw Elno,
their eyes popped out of their heads!

"You are just fabulous!" said the
jungle birds.
"The spots on your feathers are as dark
as chocolate.
Your beak is as black as night, and your
legs are as pink as the setting sun."

The jungle birds thought Elno was the most
beautiful bird in the world!
They made him sit on a rock so that
they could look at him all day.
But Elno was a shy bird.
He didn't like being looked at.

One day, Elno flapped his wings and
flew away. He went back to his hole in
the tree.
The birds were pleased to see him.
"Hey, Elno!" they said. "It's good to see you.
This place hasn't been the same
without you!"

Elno smiled and began clearing up the mess. "Home sweet home," thought Elno.